DOG DIARIES

SUNNY

DOG DIARIES

#1: GINGER
A puppy-mill survivor in search of a *furever* family

#2: BUDDY
The first Seeing Eye guide dog

#3: BARRY
Legendary rescue dog of the Great Saint Bernard Hospice

#4: TOGO
Unsung hero of the 1925 Nome Serum Run

#5: DASH
One of two dogs to travel to the New World aboard the *Mayflower*

#6: SWEETIE
George Washington's "perfect" foxhound

#7: STUBBY
One of the greatest dogs in military history

#8: FALA
"Assistant" to President Franklin Delano Roosevelt

#9: SPARKY
Fire dog veteran of the Great Chicago Fire

#10: ROLF
A tripod therapy dog

#11: TINY TIM
Canine companion to Charles Dickens, author of *A Christmas Carol*

#12: SUSAN
Matriarch of Queen Elizabeth II's corgi dynasty

#13: FIDO
Beloved family pet of Abraham Lincoln

#14: SUNNY
Pampered Peke survivor of the RMS *Titanic*

DOG DIARIES

SUNNY

BY KATE KLIMO • ILLUSTRATED BY TIM JESSELL

RANDOM HOUSE 🏠 NEW YORK

The author and editor would like to thank Raymond Lepien, Titanic Historical
Society Advisory Board, for his assistance in the preparation of this book.

Text copyright © 2019 by Kate Klimo
Cover art and interior illustrations copyright © 2019 by Tim Jessell
Photographs courtesy of Tony Davies/Shutterstock, p. ix; M Rui/FOAP/Getty Images, p. 150

Visit us on the Web! rhcbooks.com

Educators and librarians, for a variety of teaching tools, visit us at RHTeachersLibrarians.com

Library of Congress Cataloging-in-Publication Data is available upon request.
ISBN 978-0-525-64823-9 (trade pbk.) | ISBN 978-0-525-64824-6 (lib. bdg.) |
ISBN 978-0-525-64825-3 (ebook)

Printed in the United States of America

10 9 8 7 6 5 4 3 2 1

First Edition

Random House Children's Books supports the First Amendment and celebrates the right to read.

For Cousin Nathan,
who loves dogs dearly.
—K.K.

For my daughter, Molly.
She's unsinkable, too.
—T.J.

CONTENTS

1

Wednesday, April 10, 1912—
Cherbourg, France   1

2

Thursday, April 11, D Deck   20

3

Friday Morning, April 12, the Kennel   36

4

Friday Afternoon, April 12, Jenny   47

5

Friday, April 12, to Saturday, April 13,
Dogs-in-Arms   60

6

Sunday, April 14, First Class, All the Way   72

7

Sunday, April 14, 11:45 p.m.,
the Boat Deck   83

8

Monday, April 15, 12:50 a.m., the Sinking   100

9

Monday, April 15, 2:15 a.m., the Lifeboats   110

10

Monday, April 15, the *Carpathia*   118

Appendix   135

The RMS *Titanic*. Photographed at the Southampton docks, retouched to appear at sea.

Wednesday, April 10, 1912—
Cherbourg, France

If someone had told me that one day I'd be keeping a diary, I would have said, "Old boy, you must
be stark-staring mad. Me? The canine companion
of glamorous globe-trotters Mr. Henry Sleeper
Harper and his charming wife, Myra? Do I look
like some sort of owlish scribbler?" I have always
said leave the diary keeping to those ambitious,
brainy types, like border collies and pinschers. We

Pekingese are meant for finer things. No inky paws for me, thank you very much.

But that was *before* I set sail on the RMS *Titanic,* the newest, sleekest, most deluxe ship in the White Star Line fleet. On its historic maiden voyage, it was to carry us far across the ocean, from Europe to our home in New York City, in seven short days. As it turned out, that voyage gave me something to write about. More, in fact, than I could ever have imagined.

Simply *everyone* who was *anyone* was aboard. The cream of canine society. Heading up the list was the Airedale companion of the fabulously wealthy John Jacob Astor. The beloved chow chow of stockbroker Harry Anderson also had a ticket. Then there was the prize French bulldog purchased in England by banker Robert Daniel for what I hear was an indecently high price. And who could forget little Frou-Frou, that foolish little bit of fluff? I could go on, but you'll meet them all soon enough, all ten of them. Eleven, including yours truly. Eleven lucky dogs—or so we thought at the time. And let us not forget those humans aboard *without* dogs—poor lonesome souls! They just happened to number among the wealthiest humans alive, including the silver-mine queen of Colorado, Margaret Brown, and businessman Benjamin Guggenheim, a friend of the ship's captain. And have I mentioned Lady Duff-Gordon and Lady Rothes? Why, there were so many wealthy people on board, they called it "the Millionaires' Special." Sadly, as it turned out, there are some things even money cannot buy.

Titanic. There was such a bold ring to the name. Just hearing it gave me the tingles as I sat on the train that took us from Paris to the docks at Cherbourg, France. Myra was busy doing this and that with Henry, so I sat in the lap of our man, Hammad Hassat.

Hammad had joined our happy crew on a recent tour of Egypt. He was the Harpers' interpreter and guide to the wonders of that ancient land. Don't ask me what he was still doing with us (not that I minded one jot). Henry thought it would be a lark to bring Hammad back to America with us. And who, one must wonder, could possibly have need of an Egyptian interpreter in New York City? I suspect Henry wanted to be the first in his set to boast of an Egyptian manservant. That was Henry. Such a wag. (You should excuse the expression.)

Hammad was frightfully mysterious and dashingly handsome. Everywhere we went, people stared at him. But Hammad cast his eyes downward. I think he felt like an outsider. He was also sad.

And who could blame the poor dear chap? He missed his family in Cairo. I was perhaps his only friend. Wasn't he the lucky one?

Hammad, unlike me, was *not* looking forward to the voyage. The only body of water he had ever crossed before embarking on this trip was the river Nile. He was jittery on the boat from Egypt to Marseille. And the Mediterranean is a mere pond compared to the vast Atlantic Ocean.

In Paris, Hammad sent a marconigram to his brother, Said, in Cairo. He wanted to share with him the news of our upcoming voyage. (Marconigrams were the newfangled way humans sent messages to one another over long distances via a clever sort of wire.) Hammad's brother wired back to say that he foresaw the future. And what did he see? Death and destruction on the high seas. Can you imagine such a thing?

If Hammad was a Gloomy Gus, I was a ray of sunshine. At least I tried. (They don't call me Sunny for nothing!) *Old man, this voyage is going to be duck soup—you'll see,* I told Hammad. *Strictly smooth sailing!*

I said this not in so many words, of course. We Pekes aren't much for barking. (And yapping isn't really my style.) But we do have the most expressive eyes. Some say we are "all eyes."

Hammad knew and spoke many languages—including the one my eyes spoke. He understood me well. And I was equally good at reading his brooding silences. But for all my efforts to cheer him, Hammad could not shake his air of gloom and doom. Now I know why. But then I thought he was just being moody.

We arrived at the dock to find a large crowd

of fellow travelers and well-wishers. But where was the *Titanic*? A couple of tenders bobbed against the pilings: the SS *Traffic* and the SS *Nomadic*. (Don't ask me why, but humans just love to name things. Their ships, their houses, their racehorses, even their dogs—rather poorly, I might add.)

Cheer up, old chap, my eyes told Hammad. *Our trusty pals here,* Traffic *and* Nomadic, *are here to take us to the* Titanic, *no doubt.*

Hammad heaved a dispirited sigh. I could tell that he wished the *Titanic* had sailed without us.

While mates and servants piled mountains of luggage into the tenders, first-class passengers were ever so huffy. Why was there no grand ship here to meet them?

"Say, old man," Henry asked the mate assisting us in boarding the *Traffic,* "where is the *Titanic*?"

"Not to worry, sir," said the mate. "It left Southampton exactly at noon. It should be here anytime now."

While waiting, I caught sight of the Astors' Airedale, Kitty, standing between John Jacob and his young bride, Madeleine. The nerve, naming a dog Kitty! How very confusing, for one thing. And how humiliating! I don't care if you *are* the richest man on earth. Do a better job of naming your dog! Since this was hardly the dog's fault, I lifted my head and hailed her.

Ahoy there! I said.

I beg your pardon? Kitty replied.

Ahoy there, I repeated. *It's nautical talk for hello. You know—aye, aye, Captain, full speed ahead, hard to starboard . . . all that seagoing hooey.*

Brilliant! said Kitty, getting into the spirit. *Avast there, me hearty!*

All paws on the poop deck, I threw in, little knowing just how true these words would prove.

Next, I spied the jeweled collar of the toy poodle known as Frou-Frou. She rested in the arms of her doting mistress, Mrs. Helen Bishop. I have always wondered at that particular breed name, toy poodle. Make up your mind. Is it a toy or is it a dog?

Bonjour, I said (knowing she was French). *Ça va bien?*

She stuck her pointy nose in the air and cut me cold.

Well, pooh-pooh to you, too, Frou-Frou. No one could say I hadn't tried.

When I felt Hammad's fingers digging into me, I knew it was time to board the tender *Nomadic.*

Do try not to drop me in the drink, there's a good fellow. My own claws clung to his sleeve like burrs. *No water dog, I!*

I glanced over at the other tender, where the third-class passengers were also climbing aboard. One could always tell the third-class passengers by their carpetbags and their rather casual attire, whereas the second- and first-class passengers had many pieces of luggage and were decked out in all their finery. Henry wore his best bowler hat and his greased boots. Myra had donned her new Paris hat and frock and finest fur coat. (Humans, poor things, haven't much fur of their own. For warmth, they must depend upon the fur of unfortunate raccoons, rabbits, ermines, and minks. Shameful, no? But there you have it.)

To my eye, the people in the other tender seemed like jolly fine folks. But I doubt we would be doing much mingling on board the ship. On the *Titanic,* as on all means of public transportation, third-class passengers would keep to their own quarters. I know it seems snobbish and even unfair, but that's simply the way it was.

As Henry assisted Myra into the *Nomadic,*

she asked a mate, "Say, young man, is it true what they say—that the *Titanic* is unsinkable?"

"That she is, ma'am," said the mate. "They say not even God can sink the *Titanic*."

My eyes caught Hammad's. *See, old man? Nothing to worry about. Now will you stop being such a fussbudget?*

It was dusk when the order was finally given to cast off. As we moved away from the dock toward the outer harbor, the ocean swirled around us, black and oily. I shook off Said's gloomy prediction and made the best of it. Meanwhile, the humans around me chattered like magpies. Myra talked fashion with Lady Duff-Gordon. Henry discussed sailing with J. J. Astor.

I spoke with Kitty. *I'm sure you've been asked this before, but I'm dying to know. How does it feel to be the dog of the richest man in the world?*

Lucky. Kitty ducked her head. *He is such a good man. He feeds me the finest cuts of meat, drowning in gravy. It doesn't get any better. No sirree, dog!*

Gravy! I sighed wistfully. The Harpers did well by me in the meat department. But never an ounce of gravy did they offer. Gravy was my idea of dog heaven. *That sounds lovely,* I said, trying to keep the gravy envy from oozing out.

The wind soon picked up. People hunched into their collars. There was still no sign of the great ship. A nervous silence fell.

Myra spoke up. "Hand me Oogums, do, please, Hammad. Mummy needs her Oogums."

Oogums was her unfortunate pet name for yours truly. Gently, Hammad passed Oogums to Mummy. She crushed me to her breast.

"Is Mummy's wittle baby boy fwightened?" she asked me.

Easy, old girl, watch the rib cage, won't you? I'm flesh and blood, not one of your cuddly stuffed teddy bears.

"Poor, *poor* wittle Oogums must be seasick." Soon she relaxed her death grip. Eventually, I fell into a fitful doze.

An hour later, I awoke as her breast heaved with relief. I looked out over the water. A line of four tall smokestacks had appeared on the horizon. I perked up and yipped, *Ahoy there,* Titanic*! It's about time!*

Jolly good, Kitty joined in.

Even Frou-Frou managed to look enthusiastic in a toyish, poodlish kind of way.

We heard a round of rowdy cheering from the passengers on the other boat.

As we passed into the shadow of the great ship, the waters churned. I heard the steady rumble of its mighty engines. I saw clouds of steam billowing skyward from its smokestacks. In spite of its enormous size, it seemed to float weightlessly on the water, ten elegant decks stacked up like the floors of the finest hotel you could imagine. Its lights were blazing and its brass-work sparkled, and I heard music playing from somewhere. Kitty lifted her muzzle and began to yowl.

"Hush, Kitty," said her mistress. "She likes to sing," she explained to the other passengers.

Sing, shming, said I. *She obviously hates music. Can't you see it hurts her ears?* Humans, sadly, are often without a clue when it comes to their canine companions.

From an upper deck, a mate lowered a wooden gangway, and one of our crew made it fast to the tender.

I watched as the men hoisted the luggage using a crane. It dangled over my head. If it fell, my face would be flatter than thousands of years of breeding had already made it.

I was relieved when Myra handed me back to Hammad. I buried my head in his chest. Soon I felt him making his steady way across the rickety bridge.

On deck, the officers were lined up in spiffy navy uniforms with gold trim. Quite the row of popinjays.

One of them stepped forward and said, "Welcome aboard the RMS *Titanic*. It's a pleasure to serve you." He snapped a salute.

Myra said, "Are you the captain of this ship, young man?"

He replied, "No, madam, I am not. Captain Smith is rather busy just now on the bridge. Allow me to do the honors. I am the ship's chief purser,

Hugh Walter McElroy, at your service."

Then Myra put to him the question she apparently never tired of asking: "I want the truth, Mr. Purser. Is this ship really unsinkable?"

"Solid as a rock, ma'am. But why take my word for it?" he said. "Here is Mr. Thomas Andrews, he who designed the *Titanic*."

He gestured to a slender young man standing nearby. He was peering hard at something on the wall and scribbling furiously on a pad of paper.

"Mr. Andrews," the purser said to the man with the pad, "tell the lady that this ship is perfect."

The man looked up nervously. "Well, *almost* perfect. I see now there are too many screws in the coatracks. And the Reading and Writing Room may be overlarge. And there's too much starch in the first-class dining saloon linen napkins." He stopped himself and grinned. "But she's unsinkable, my lady, rest assured."

Myra beamed.

Moments later, a bevy of bellboys made off with our luggage while we followed a steward, who treated us to a short tour. We viewed the dining saloon, the library, several rather posh restaurants, and the Reading and Writing Room. Up on what they called the boat deck was a fully equipped gymnasium. A chap in white flannels bounded over to us and introduced himself as Thomas W. McCauley, physical instructor.

The Harpers oohed and aahed over the shining rows of equipment: the spanking-new ranks of machines to row with and weights to lift. There were bicycles that went nowhere and saddles and stirrups on mechanical horses. Why, there was even a mechanical camel! What would they think of next? A dog-nasium?

The steward then asked if we would be interested in visiting the swimming facilities, the Turkish bath, and the squash courts, all located on the lower decks. Myra rolled her eyes, and Henry assured him that we would get around to viewing everything in time.

Following our tour, we glided down a wide double staircase beneath a domed skylight, from which hung a crystal chandelier. On the wall, a stately clock ticked away the seconds. Everything from the gold on the clock to the polish on the bannisters gleamed and sparkled.

The *Titanic* was one fine ship. Cracking fine!

THURSDAY, APRIL 11, D DECK

There was a flurry of activity when we arrived at our stateroom, number 33 on D Deck. Hammad had just gone to inspect his own private cabin nearby. Myra and Henry fussed as the bellboys unpacked the trunks, leaving me at liberty to explore.

We had two bedrooms, two walk-in closets, and a parlor, which would no doubt be my personal doggie den. The fittings were excellent. Brocade on the walls. Thick carpeting on the floors.

Heavy drapes at the windows. Everywhere were beautifully upholstered chairs and tables and sofas. Everything tip-top.

Hammad returned with a new officer, one we hadn't met before. While giving me a rather snooty look, the officer said he wished to speak with the Harpers. The Harpers, emerging from the bedroom, listened to what he had to say and grew increasingly upset. He was apologetic but firm. Myra darted a helpless glance in my direction. This did not bode well.

It seemed I was to be banished from this Eden of velvet cushions and plush carpets. I was to stay in the ship's kennel! And why? Because the *Titanic* rules were clear, the officer said—no animals allowed in the staterooms. Really? And I, with a first-class ticket? The idea!

Myra stood her ground. "But I know I saw

Liz Rothschild take her Pom into her room."

"I wouldn't know anything about that," said the officer uneasily.

"And I *distinctly* heard Mrs. Bishop say she was permitted to keep her dog in her stateroom."

The officer sighed. "Aye, that's true. It was thought that Frou-Frou was too delicate to be left in the kennel with the other dogs."

Too delicate? What am I? I asked with my eyes. *The Hunchback of Notre-Dame?*

"You're lucky, ma'am, that your dog doesn't have to travel in cargo with the roosters and cockerels and canaries. We've a right deluxe kennel on the boat deck."

Myra looked faint. "And am I expected to climb untold flights of stairs every time I wish to visit my Oogums?"

"Madam, you may be spared the labor of

mounting or descending the stairs by entering one of the smoothly gliding elevators located for your convenience in front of the Grand Staircase. And rest assured that Sun Yat-sen will be in excellent hands."

As if being banished to a kennel wasn't galling enough! The man was now using the name on my registration papers! Sun Yat-sen. You see, being of Chinese origin, I was named for the president of China. But *no one* ever called me that. I was Sunny to all my nearest and dearest, among whom I clearly did not count this villain.

"You and your pet may visit together on the promenade deck," said the villain. "Rest assured. He will be taken out for regular walks and airings."

Airings? As if I were a piece of bedding rather than a purebred Pekingese! And besides, everyone knew I hated to walk. I preferred to be carried.

The officer continued: "The kennel sits snug up against the fourth funnel, so it is amply cozy. One of our butchers will personally be providing the dogs with the very finest cuts of meat. Our four-legged passengers are very important to us."

My lady perked up. "Did you hear dat, Oogums?" She lifted me beneath the armpits, which I hated. We were nose to nose. "You'll be warm and toasty-woasty, and you'll dine in the style my itty-wittle prince deserves."

Oh, please. I turned my head aside. *Spare me the baby talk. Just take me away and let's get this tiresome business over with.*

Hammad was good enough to carry me up to the kennel. Knowing I was miffed, he stroked me steadily—for all the good it did. I am not so easily consoled.

High up on the boat deck, where the sea breeze

ran through me like a sword, the officer swung open a little door. Inside, I smelled dog. Correction: make that unhappy dog. With a sinking heart, I saw the reason why. The dogs were imprisoned in a row of lowly cages. This was even worse than I thought it would be.

"Hello, doggies," said the officer with a note of false cheer in his voice. "I've brought you a new play pal. His name is Sun Yat-sen."

I received a welcome of snuffles and growls.

Hammad set me down in an empty cage. He gave me a farewell pat and fastened the latch.

Be a good little gent, his eyes said.

I shall try, my own eyes replied.

The officer and Hammad took their leave and closed the door.

The French bulldog to my left chuckled. *Sun Yat-sen? Surely you jest.*

You may call me Sunny, I said, feeling ever so slightly miffed. *And your name is . . . ?*

He shifted uneasily. *I am a highly prized French bulldog. The name is Gamin de Pycombe.*

Hmmmm, talk about silly names. What do your friends call you?

I haven't many of those. He sniffed.

Well then, I said, feeling sorry for the wretch.

What do you say we call you Guy?

I think it suits him, said Kitty. *Hi, Guy.*

The Astor Airedale occupied the cage across from mine. It was some consolation that even the dog of the wealthiest man on earth was subject to the *Titanic's* ridiculous no-dogs-in-cabins rule.

Hi, Guy, chimed in all the other dogs.

Who else do we have here? said I, looking up and

down the row of cages. *Howl out your names loud and clear so I know who my fellow inmates are.*

To my right loomed a slobbering Great Dane. Even in a cage twice as big as the rest of us had, he still looked as cramped as a large ship in a too-tiny bottle. *My lady, Ann Elizabeth Isham, calls me Darling Boy,* he said.

I nodded. *Pleased to meet you, Darling Boy.*

I turned to the chow next to him. *And your name, my good fellow?*

Chow, he said.

I could see this fine fellow was a tad thick. *Yes, your black tongue tells me your breed, but what is your name?*

Chow, he said. *It's my breed* and *it's my name.*

I sighed. Yet another ridiculous human name for dog-kind. *Well,* said I, looking on the bright side, *at least it will be easy to remember.*

My name's easy to remember, too, said the fox ter-rier next to Chow. *My master, William Dulles, calls me Dog.*

Honestly! Kitty, Dog, Chow? What next, Poochie? Or perhaps *Canis familiaris*? Some hu-mans had an appalling lack of imagination.

The occupant of the cage next to Dog's was as fluffy as a lady's mink muff. She looked familiar. *Haven't we met?* I asked her. *Don't tell me. You're Elizabeth Rothschild's Pomeranian? Rothschild of the Watkins Glen Rothschilds, that is. Not to be mistaken for the banking Rothschilds. In any case, I never forget a Pom. But I was told Elizabeth smuggled you into her stateroom. What are you doing here?*

Dog spoke up. *You've got it all wrong. This little lady belongs to Margaret Hays. She's French, aren't you, mademoiselle?*

Oui, zat I am. I am called Lily. I do not speak zee

Doggie-English so good. Mees Margaret bought me in Paris. And now I find I am leaving my beloved homeland for America. It is too, too tragique!

Cheer up, I told her. *America's a swell place. You're lucky she isn't dragging you to Egypt, like my humans did with me. Egypt was rough going. In Cairo, there were rats running around the Pyramids who were bigger than I was.*

I'll have you know, old fellow, that there are rats running around this ship, said Guy.

No! we all woofed in disbelief.

Say it is not so! Lily wailed.

Oh, but it is, said Guy.

That just goes to show you that even brand-spanking-new ships have rats, said I.

It's all the delicious food in the Titanic *larders,* said Guy. *The rats smell it. Can't you?*

And how! said Kitty. *Mutton and lamb chops.*

Sausages and stinky cheeses, said Dog, licking his lips. I like the sound of that.

Whole sides of beef and kidneys! said Chow, drooling.

And what about zee favorite of zee French, pâté de foie gras? said Lily.

Rub-a-dub-dub, give us some grub! sang out yet another Airedale and a Cavalier King Charles spaniel, who shared the cage on the very end.

Stop! howled Darling Boy. *All this talk of food is making my stomach gurgle.*

We all paused to listen, and sure enough: the great dog's gut gurgled and popped to rival the very engines of the *Titanic.*

Anyone have anything else to talk about other than rats and food? I asked.

Chow piped up. *I hear somebody was planning to ship one hundred English foxhounds, but they canceled at the last minute. Can you imagine sharing these quarters with a hundred foxhounds?*

This whole ship isn't big enough for a hundred foxhounds, I said. *All that yipping and yapping and tallyhoing. And even without the foxhounds, it's too crowded in here. Say, I've got a ripping-good idea. Let's break out of this joint and have ourselves some real fun.*

There followed a good deal of canine hemming and hawing.

Perish the thought, my good man, said Guy.

Oh, we would never! said the King Charles.

Never, ever, ever, said his Airedale cellmate. *We two are the cherished dogs of the Carter family children, and we obey the rules.*

As do I! said the Astor Airedale.

I'm staying put! boomed Darling Boy. *Ann's bound to come looking for me, and if I'm not here, she'll be awfully upset. We're very attached, you see.*

I think I speak for most of us, said Dog, *when I say that we are well-bred, obedient dogs. If our people put us down here, I'm sure they know what's best.*

I was disappointed but not surprised. Most dogs are faithful to a fault. *Very well*, I said. *Then it's every dog for himself. But don't come whining to me when your bladder bursts because some bellboy forgot to "air" you!*

Suddenly, the kennel door swung open.

The small personage who stood framed against the light could only be described with two words: *street* and *urchin*. He was small and scrawny, in need of a bath, and shabbily dressed. But the cap sitting rakishly atop his shaggy head hinted at a certain sense of style. As his eyes roved up and down the cages, they widened in wonder.

"I came looking for me good pal Jenny, and here I find me a mess of doggies instead!" said he. "They didn't tell me there'd be dogs on this tub. I love dogs." He pulled a sad face. "Had to leave me mutt behind in Belfast with me great-aunt Katie."

My fellow inmates shrank back into their cages. But I stood my ground. He might have been a little rough around the edges, but his eyes were soft. Maybe, like my friend Hammad, he would understand me.

I moved to the edge of my cage and pressed my

flat face to the bars. I whimpered in what I hoped was an appealing way.

The boy knelt down and pushed his grubby knuckle through the bars. "What in the world kind of dog are you? You look like a wee lion, you do. Can you roar for me, little lion dog?"

My eyes said, *If you'll lift the latch on my cage, I'll roar like the Hound of the Baskervilles.*

But before I could open my mouth to give it a shot, a man's voice sounded from out in the hall.

"*There* you be, Frankie, me boy. I been looking all over tarnation for you. I mighta known you'd gone to the dogs. Help your uncles and me get sorted down in our cabin, and *then* you can monkey about all you like."

"Righty-o, Dad! See you mutts later," he said, giving my nose a gentle pinch.

And then my urchin was gone!

Friday Morning, April 12, the Kennel

I awoke in the morning to the faint sound of crowing. For a moment, I thought I had died and gone to the Great Barnyard in the Sky. But it was just the roosters' ruckus traveling up from the lower depths.

And then I remembered, high up on this ship as I now was, how far I had come down in the world since yesterday. While my people were no doubt enjoying mutton chops and gravy with their shirred eggs, their beloved Peke was being served a bowl of slop. Actually, the meat wasn't bad. It was veal. But where, pray tell, was the gravy?

So far, I had not met the good man responsible for this establishment, said to be one of their best butchers. He sent others to serve the meat scraps. After breakfast, a small army of boys took us out for our "airing" two decks down on the poop deck. (Please, no jokes.) Hastily, they walked us around. Hastily, we did our business. Then one of the boys came along and swept our business into the deep blue sea. After which we were rushed back into our cages. Pretty pathetic airing, if you ask me.

In due time, a lovely lady dropped by the kennel. Darling Boy greeted her with a hearty *woof*, rocking and thumping his cage in his eagerness to get out.

"You poor, dear creature! I'm going to demand

that Mr. Hutchinson find you a bigger crate. And if he doesn't, you're staying in my cabin. That's all there is to it!" When the lady set Darling Boy free, he nearly bowled her over in his excitement.

I missed you, Miss Ann! With his huge, slobbery tongue, he licked her face, and she laughed in delight. "I missed you, too, boy!" She attached a lead to his collar stout enough to tow a rowboat. "Come along now and let's stretch those legs."

The rest of us watched as the lucky boy romped off at the side of his adoring mistress. Soon Mr. Robert Daniel came to claim his prize bulldog.

So long, lads and lassies, Guy told us as he waddled off.

Not long after that, the Carter children, Billy and Lucy, burst in upon us.

"P.U.," said Billy, holding his nose. "It stinks to high heaven in here."

"Billy," his sister scolded. "Don't be rude. These dogs can't help it if they're cooped up in a windowless little room all day. Poor little beasts."

But did she lift a finger to free the poor little beasts? Not on your life. The children simply made off with their Airedale and King Charles, whose names I never did catch. After they had trotted off, those of us who remained dozed in our cages like zoo animals.

I wondered why Hammad had not come for me. Didn't Myra miss her Oogums? Or were they all too seasick to pay me any mind? Somehow, I doubted it. The Atlantic Ocean that morning was as smooth as a millpond, the sky just as blue as a china plate. Beneath me, I felt the *Titanic*'s mighty engines churning away. Oh, would that we were nearing the end of our voyage rather than just starting out!

And then, as suddenly as he disappeared yesterday, the urchin boy, Frankie, was back! I shuffled over to the bars to greet him.

He unlatched the door to my cage. I leapt into his waiting arms and licked his hands in thanks.

"What do you say to a wee stroll about the ship, little lion dog? I'm looking for a friend of mine. Her name is Jenny. You can keep me company."

I like the sound of that, old boy. Let's look for her in first class, I told him with wide, eager eyes. My curly tail wagged.

He pointed a suspicious finger at me. "Is that a smile on your face? I've never seen a dog smile before."

Sunny is as sunny does, my eyes told him.

"Come on, then. What're we waitin' for?"

He got up and sprang to the door.

I moved not a hair.

Frankie turned and looked back at me, hands on hips. "What's the matter with ye? Ye don't like to walk? Fancy that! A doggie who won't walk." Then it dawned on him. "You want to be toted about like a wee pasha. You're not exactly a Paddy longlegs, are you? A mite on the stubby side, those legs of yours."

No need to hurl insults. I can't help it if I was bred to be carried around in the sleeves of Chinese royals.

He took off his shabby little jacket and wrapped it around me. Then he lifted me and tied the jacket snugly around his shoulders.

So long, friends! I said to the others as Frankie toted me off like a peddler in his pack.

A chorus of barks, yips, and gurgles bade us farewell.

Once again, I found myself out in the open sea air. Next to us loomed that fourth smokestack.

I felt the heat of it on my whiskers.

He pointed toward the front of the vessel. "That's called the bow. The bridge is up there. The captain's the boss of the ship, and that's where he steers it. This is the boat deck." Frankie pointed to rows of boats, covered in canvas. "In Belfast, I lived near the shipyards where they built this tub.

Me uncles labored on it. I was a wharf rat. I know every inch of this tub. These be the lifeboats," he said. "Jenny loves to take naps in the lifeboats."

What an odd place for a little girl to take a nap. Didn't she have a cabin with a bunk?

Frankie went from boat to boat, peering beneath the canvas. "Funny thing," he said. "There are more than twenty-two hundred folks aboard this ship. It's like a small city. There are fourteen lifeboats and two emergency cutters—they swing out and drop into the drink in case some poor soul falls overboard. Even if you count the four collapsible boats, there's nowhere near enough boats."

Then he waved a hand. "But, hey, we don't need 'em, do we? The *Titanic*'s unsinkable, so these're just for show. *And* for Jenny to nap in. But not today, I guess."

He pointed toward the bow to a high mast with a bucket halfway up it big enough to hold two men. "That's the crow's nest," he told me. "Them two fellers is on watch duty. They can see whales and dolphins and sea lions from up there. There's a ladder leading up to it inside the mast. Jenny can climb, too, but not up there, she wouldn't. It would make the watchmen too nervous. Maybe I'll climb up there someday. See me some whales."

From a doorway nearby, we heard a steady clicking sound. Frankie walked over and peered in. We found a small room crammed with equipment. A man sat at a desk piled high with paper. There were cups over his ears and his finger nervously stabbed at a golden key. *Clickety. Clickety. Clickety.*

He looked like the person Hammad visited in Paris to wire his brother, Said. This, I wagered, was the ship's wireman, in charge of sending marconigrams.

"How's it going, mister?" Frankie asked the man.

He looked up, startled, fumbling off his ear cups.

"Every person aboard this vessel wants to send a message to all their friends and relatives. And they all say the same thing: 'Dear So-and-So, I'm aboard the *Titanic* and having the time of my life. Wish you were here.' It's enough to keep me and my associate, Mr. Bride, busy twenty-four hours a day. My finger's already cramping up."

My eye strayed to a half-open curtain. On the other side, in another small room, a man lay on a narrow bunk. Mr. Bride—I presumed—snored soundly.

The man on duty gave Frankie a long narrow look. "Say," he said, "you'd best be getting back below to your proper place, little mister."

"I was looking for Jenny," Frankie told him.

The man eased off a bit and smiled. "So it's Jenny you're after, is it? Last I saw her, she was headed for the boiler room. You know our Jenny. She craves the heat. Especially these days."

4

FRIDAY AFTERNOON, APRIL 12, JENNY

Down, down, down the steep stairs we went until we came out on a narrow hallway lined with doors.

Frankie said, "I thought we'd make a wee stop-over on our way to the engine room." Halfway down the corridor, he opened a door. "This is me very own cabin," he said proudly.

It was a small room barely big enough for four narrow bunks. No carpets, velvet, or brocade here. Three of the four bunks held snoring bodies.

"Me dad and me uncles," Frankie explained in a whisper. "They was up all night, playing cards. Them bunks is a lot comfier than me lumpy bed at home, which we had to share. In America, we'll sleep on feather beds." He closed the door and continued down the hall toward the sound of music and people talking and laughing.

"I want you to meet me big sister. She wants to have a small doggie of her own someday, like all them fancy society ladies."

At the end of the hall, we came to a large, noise-filled room. Frankie said, "This is the third-class lounge."

The furnishings were decent but plain—wooden tables and benches. A bartender stood behind a long bar crowded with people drinking and shouting over the music. A makeshift band sat off to one side playing hand organs, fiddles, and bagpipes. Kitty would not have been pleased with the racket, but I found it rather charming. The dance floor was chockablock with couples dancing. These days, the smart set—those folks up in first class—were doing a stiff-limbed dance called the turkey trot. But people down here danced a loose and lively sort of jig.

A pretty young woman broke away and danced over to greet us. "What's this, baby brother? A teddy bear for me?"

"It ain't no such thing," said Frankie. "He's a little lion dog."

Her eyes widened. "Go on with you, Frankie! That's some fine lady's pocketbook dog. You'll get into a world of trouble when the owner finds you've made off with it."

Frankie shrugged. "I just borrowed him, like, for a bit of a lark."

"Best finish your lark and return him," she said. "She'll be frantic by now. I know I would be if he were mine," she added, giving me a longing look.

A small crowd gathered around us. People reached out and stroked me. I wasn't afraid. Their voices were friendly and their hands were warm.

"That's a mighty strange-looking animal," a woman said. "Comical."

"Noble is more like it," a man said. "Mark my word. He's an aristocrat."

"Yeah? Bet he's worth a king's ransom," another said.

"You take good care of this little dog," said Frankie's sister. Her eyes took on a dreamy look. "Maybe in America, I'll get me my own pocket-book dog to carry about on me arm."

"I'm sure you will, Sis," Frankie said. "Come on, little lion dog. Let's go down to the engine room and see if Jenny's keeping company with the stokers and greasers."

A steep stairway led us down to the very bottom of the ship. Down here, the noise of the engines pounded against my ears. The air was hot and heavy and close. I felt the weight of the upper decks pressing upon my skull. My heart fluttered in my chest, and I panted.

You're a long way from first class now, Sunny boy, I told myself. If Frankie's girlfriend, Jenny, was down here, she was made of sterner stuff than I. Meanwhile, Frankie whistled cheerfully as he marched through a series of empty compartments. The compartments were divided by heavy doors. Frankie had to use all his might to open and close them.

"These doors is called hatches." Frankie raised his voice over the clanking of the engines.

"Bulkheads divide the compartments. A bulkhead means a barrier. If one of them gets a hole punched in it and fills up with water, the other compartments stay dry. That's what makes this tub unsinkable. That and her double bottom. But if you ask me, the sea's bigger and stronger than any ship, and it's got a mind of its own. If it wants to sink ye, ye won't stand a chance, no matter how many chambers and bulkheads and double-walled keels ye may have. That's what I think."

Finally, we arrived at a great cavern of a room filled with enormous, clanking machines. The heat and noise were now almost unbearable. A team of brawny men toiled. Some read dials and made markings on pads. Others scrambled here and there, polishing the machinery until it sparkled and shone.

"These are the greasers!" Frankie had to shout

now to be heard. "They make sure the engines run smooth. The *Titanic*'s got all kinds of newfangled engines."

From there, we moved into what Frankie told me was the boiler room. Here, with muscles bulging, men shoveled coal to feed the flames in a row of raging furnaces. It was alarmingly hot. Hot enough to singe my fur.

"These are the stokers!"

One of the men stopped and leaned on his shovel. He took out a rag and wiped the sweat from his brow. Frankie went on. "This tub has a hundred and fifty-nine furnaces. They fuel twenty-nine boilers! The boilers heat the water and turn it to steam. The steam powers the engines, which turn the ship's three propellers. You can't see them. They're on the outside of the hull. Big as windmills, they are."

I'm sure this is all very impressive, but may we please leave? I growled testily. Frankie's back was damp with sweat. If you must know, dogs sweat, too. But only on those areas not covered with fur. Like the pads of our paws. Mine happened to be sweating buckets. *Buckets,* I tell you.

The stoker seemed to sense my discomfort. "Might be too hot down here for that little dog of yours," he said.

By now, I was panting so rapidly I felt faint. Frankie said, "We're looking for Jenny. The wire-man said she might be down here."

"That she was," said the stoker, "but it didn't seem to suit her. She liked the heat, but I don't think she cared much for the noise."

Frankie nodded thoughtfully. "Hah! I think I know where she went," he said. "Come on, little lion. Let's get you out of here. See you around!" Frankie waved to the stoker.

As we moved back up to the higher decks, the air began to cool. Bit by bit, I revived. Soon we were walking down a corridor along which wafted the delicious smell of baking bread.

A woman carrying a covered tray pushed through a swinging door and came toward us.

"Is Jenny in there?" Frankie asked her.

"Aye," said the woman. "And her time's come and gone. You'll find her in back. We gave her a nice nest of rags."

Poor Jenny! In rags and tatters! No cabin, no bed, no proper clothing? This was worse than I expected.

Frankie pushed through the door into the biggest kitchen I'd ever seen. It was warm in here, but pleasantly so, and alive with delicious smells. There was an entire wall of ovens and stoves. Men in white hats and aprons were cooking and frying and baking away. One man was kneading a big pile of dough. A second man was scooping loaves of bread out of an oven with a wooden paddle. With a gloved hand, a third was unloading golden-brown rolls from a big pan into silver baskets. Frankie reached for a roll, and the man slapped his hand.

Frankie grinned. "Pretty please?"

The man growled and tossed him one. Frankie caught it. He broke off a piece and offered it to me, then crammed the rest into his maw. I'm not usually one for bread, but this buttery morsel tasted heavenly.

Frankie told the man through a full mouth, "We're looking for Jenny."

The man jutted his chin toward the far corner.

"Over yonder. But mind you don't bother her. She's busy with important matters."

Between the last stove and a heaping pile of coal, a big orange-striped cat lay in a nest of clean rags. Six tiny newborn kittens suckled at her side.

"Hello, Jenny!" said Frankie. "We been searching all over the ship for ye."

Jenny let out a steady rumbling purr. *Hello, yourself, Frankie, me boy. You're a sight for sore eyes.*

Well now, didn't I feel foolish? Here I had been thinking that Jenny was a rather poorly off *human girl,* and she was a happy and contented *mother cat.* So Frankie was one of those humans who liked both dogs and cats!

"Jenny, this is my new friend, little lion dog. Don't worry. He's nice and gentle." Frankie knelt down. "Your kittens are beautiful, Jenny, just like you. Can I have one when it gets big enough?"

She blinked up at him. *I'll save the biggest and best of the litter for you, Frankie, me boy.*

Madam, I said to Jenny the cat, *I believe congratulations are in order. That's a lovely batch of kittens.*

Thank you, sir, said Jenny. *I almost didn't make it here in time. I was planning to have my litter down in the engine room. But at the last moment, I got out. I didn't care for it.*

I don't blame you a bit, I said. *All those big, burly men. All that noise. And it was as hot as blazes.*

It wasn't the men or the noise or heat, she said. *It just didn't feel like a safe place for me and my young 'uns.*

But haven't you heard? I said. *This ship's perfectly safe. Why, it's unsinkable.*

Jenny heaved a sigh. *Not at the rate it's going now. Can't you hear the engines? They're straining— being pushed to the limit. You'd think the captain was trying to break some sort of speed record. If he's not careful, he'll break the ship instead of the record. But these captains are all alike, racing through the ice fields, heedless of the danger. It's just a matter of time before one of them meets the business end of a glacier.*

Just what I needed to hear: more glum predictions. But I hadn't met all that many cats. Perhaps cats were just naturally nervous and gloomy and there was nothing whatsoever to worry about. Or so I hoped.

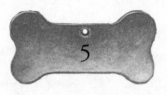

FRIDAY, APRIL 12, TO SATURDAY, APRIL 13, DOGS-IN-ARMS

By the time Frankie returned me to the kennel, I was limp and tired. Unwrapping me from his jacket, he set me back in my cage. He fluffed up my fur, which was fearfully matted.

Brushing the dog hair off his jacket, he said, "I'm surprised ye have any fur left on your wee body." He grinned. Then he leaned down and pressed his finger gently to my nose.

"Sleep tight, little lion. Same time tomorrow, eh? We'll visit Jenny and the kittens and then do us a tad more exploring."

I shall look forward to it, old boy, my eyes told him as my new friend departed.

I sighed and lay down with an exhausted little snort.

You look a fright, said Kitty.

Enfin! said Lily. *We had begun to worry zat zee urchin had made off wiz you for good.*

Where have you been all this time? asked Dog.

Here and there, touring the ship . . . seeing how the other half lives, I told them.

Lily shuddered delicately. *How ghastly.*

It's not as bad as you think. The people in third class might not have money. But they sure know how to have a good time. Say, have my people come to visit me?

Nope, said the Chow. *It looks like we've been left high and dry.*

I can't say I felt the least bit upset. Let them stay away, for all I cared. I had found in Frankie a friend—and from the most unlikely of places, third class!

The next morning, I found the roosters' crowing quaint and endearing. The meat scraps served up to us by the kitchen scullion were very tasty (even if they weren't swimming in gravy). And the morning airing was downright delightful. I was looking forward to my next adventure with young Frankie, when Hammad showed his handsome face.

Pride prevented me from wagging my tail.

Well, look who the cat dragged in, I said with my eyes.

Do not ask, my friend, his look told me.

The Egyptian appeared less than his usual spiffy self. His hair was out of order, and there was a small spot on his collar.

His eyes were brimming with apology. He said aloud, "They kept me busy yesterday. But today, Madam wants to make sure she spends time with you. She doesn't care what the rules say. She is feeling like quite the rebel."

Well, well, well, I said. *It's about time.*

I bid my fellow inmates a fond farewell. I wondered, fleetingly, about Frankie. When he came for me, would he be dashed with disappointment to find me gone? Or would he whistle and be on his merry way?

After stopping on the poop deck for a *you-know-what,* Hammad and I ascended to A Deck. In the Reading and Writing Room, men read books and newspapers. In the first-class lounge, little girls sat on the floor playing with dolls. Young Bobo Dodge ran a toy car along the floor. No one here was drinking or laughing or playing music or dancing jigs as they had been down in the third-class lounge. It was all frightfully dull. Nor was Myra anywhere to be seen.

We proceeded down to B Deck. Here, we came upon a large, airy room with windows overlooking sea and sky. It was furnished with wicker tables and chairs and benches. There were potted plants with shiny leaves climbing up trellises. At one of the round tables, Mrs. Margaret Brown, the silver-mine queen, presided over a game of gin rummy with her lady friends. And at a nearby table sat Myra.

"Oogums!" She welcomed me with arms wide-spread.

Gathering me up, she rubbed noses with me. "I've missed ooh. Did Oogums miss Mummy?"

I've been wasting away. My eyes told the lie that she longed to read there.

Sharing a table with her were Frou-Frou and her mistress, Helen Bishop. Mrs. Astor was also there but without Kitty. Poor thing was still a prisoner of the doggie dungeon.

A man sitting at a nearby table was glaring at us. At me in particular, it seemed. Whatever was his problem?

Helen leaned in to the other two ladies. "That is Mr. Millet, the famous painter. I hear he disapproves of society ladies and our small dogs."

"He thinks we treat them like accessories," said Mrs. Astor.

Myra raised an eyebrow. "Oogums *is* an accessory," she said. "The very finest money can buy."

Like the accessory that I was, I lay in her arms and basked in her affections. The ladies chatted away about frocks and hats and who was summering where in the coming season. Ho hum.

My eye drifted to the shiny leaves growing up the nearby trellis and to the pot from which they had sprung. I felt an irresistible urge to shock Mamzelle Frou-Frou.

Pssssst. What would you do if I were to hop off this lap and go wee-wee on that plant?

Frou-Frou's little mouth dropped open. *No!*

And why not? I asked. *Isn't that what the Lord Dog put potted plants on this earth for?*

Please, sir! Frou-Frou gasped. *You shock me to my very core.*

Do you want to hear something even more shocking? You'll never guess where I was yesterday.

She couldn't guess. *Tell me,* she said.

Down in the engine room, I said, *with the stokers and the greasers.*

She was agog. *Say it isn't true! I hear there is the very worst element down there. The dregs of society.*

I became aware of Myra speaking. "I had a talk with one of the officers earlier. He says the dogs are getting along famously in the kennel. They're actually planning to hold a dog show on Monday. Isn't that charming? You can't wait, can you, Oogums?"

A dog show? Really? What next? A fox hunt on the promenade deck? What folly!

"I think we all know who will win, don't we?" said Helen, holding out Frou-Frou like a small trophy she had already won.

"Tut-tut. I'm not so sure about that," said Myra. "My Sunny's conformation is perfect in every way."

Oh, dear lady, you have no idea how perfect. They loved me in steerage.

"I wonder, is there a dog groomer on board?" Mrs. Astor asked.

"How can there not be?" said Myra. "There's everything else a respectable person could need. There's a barbershop and a beauty salon."

"And a Turkish bath and a heated swimming bath," added Helen.

"Why not a dog groomer?" said Myra airily.

"I'll have to ask Hammad to make an appointment for Oogums."

I rolled my eyes at Frou-Frou. *Oh, great joy in the morning! The only thing I enjoy more than a grooming is a good worming.*

Too true, said Frou-Frou.

Briefly, I am happy to write, the toy poodle and the Peke shared a rare moment of unity.

Suddenly, we heard a loud commotion from the deck outside.

Mrs. Astor leapt to her feet and clapped a hand over her heart. "I knew it! Something's gone wrong with the ship!"

Clutching their canine accessories, Helen and Myra followed her and the other people in the café out onto the deck.

A large crowd of people had gathered at the rail, looking down at the third-class well deck below.

People shouted and pointed. Some of them, like the silver-mine queen, laughed in delight. Others frowned in disapproval. Someone was swinging from the cable on the luggage crane in the well deck.

"Why, it's a little boy!" Helen cried out in amazement.

The boy swung wide and pulled himself up to stand on top of the crane. He was nearly eye level with those of us in first class. There he stood, balancing, arms wide, grinning proudly.

Myra said, "Who does he think he is? The Daring Young Man on the Flying Trapeze?"

It was Frankie! He did a neat backflip and landed on his feet on the well deck, where yet another crowd of gawkers had gathered.

"Well done, you!" Margaret Brown called out as she tossed him a gold coin.

Frankie caught it out of the air.

The crowd clapped as he swept a bow. When he lifted his head, he spotted me. Winking, he gave me a cocky thumbs-up.

"Ill-mannered youth," Myra sniffed.

Ah, but this boy had something more important than manners. He had spirit.

A man parted the crowd and growled, "You little monkey, you'd better start running! And if I catch you doing that again, I'll tan your hide!"

"I do believe that's Mr. Bailey, one of the masters-at-arms," someone said. "That lad's in for a world of trouble now."

But not even a master-at-arms could catch my Frankie. Laughing, he dived into the nearest open door, like a genie going back into his bottle.

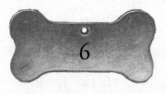

Sunday, April 14,
First Class, All the Way

I spent a lovely stolen night with the Harpers in their stateroom instead of with the exiles up in the kennel. Before this moment, I had taken such luxury as my due. Never again.

In the morning, we remained snug as bugs in rugs inside our suite. Henry was feeling lazy. And Myra saw no reason to get dressed and go out. Rumor had it that the captain had canceled the lifeboat drill because it was too cold.

Myra lolled against her pillows in her best bed jacket and pouted. "We don't need a drill, anyway."

Cold or not, there were some drills that were absolutely necessary—even urgent, one might say. Like, for instance, taking one's dog outside to do his business. I was relieved when Hammad came to the door. At least *someone* was thinking of my needs.

Thank you! my eyes told him.

Once outside, I was less thankful. It was cold enough to freeze the pee on the poop deck. Not that Hammad seemed to notice. Being from Egypt, he was normally quite sensitive to the cold. But today, his unbuttoned coat flapped in the wind as he wandered the decks with me nestled in his arms.

We soon wandered down to D Deck. The first-class dining saloon, with its bank of stained glass windows, looked bright and cheery inside, but Hammad made no move to enter.

When the door swung open, we spied the captain himself, a tall man with a white beard, standing before a small gathering of passengers. They listened as dutifully as small children as he read to them from a book.

Two stewards joined us, taking a break. The first one said, "That might be the last Sunday sermon the captain ever delivers."

The second one nodded. "Rumor has it he'll be retiring at the end of this voyage."

"The *Titanic*'s a grand vessel. I'd say it's a fitting way to end a grand career," said the first.

"So far, the voyage has gone smooth as silk," said the second.

The first: "Yeah, but there's icebergs been reported, you know."

The second: "There's always icebergs in the North Atlantic. Captain'll handle it. He always does."

The stewards finished their break and hustled off to their duties.

Hammad sighed and shook his head. This conversation did not exactly do wonders for his jittery nerves. He walked over to the rail and looked back at the wake foaming behind us. It seemed that Jenny the cat was right. The captain *was* speeding. And supposedly through a field of icebergs, no less.

Hammad and I scanned the horizon. I had never seen one of these icebergs with my own eyes. But I assumed they were just large chunks of ice floating in the water like an ever-so-much-thicker version of the shaved ice in a Punch Romaine.

As the morning stretched into the afternoon, the day grew colder still. Even so, Hammad continued to roam the decks, using me for a hand warmer.

Most of the passengers had chosen to stay inside, cozy in their cabins or in the various lounges, where they played cards and read or wrote. There was no sign so far today of Frankie. I imagined him tucked up in his little cabin playing cards with his father and uncles. Or perhaps he was keeping company with Jenny and the kittens and nibbling on rolls warm from the oven. I'll say this about Frankie. He knew how to take care of himself.

We watched as two lookouts popped up in the crow's nest. Their heads were wrapped in woolen scarves.

"Let's hope they are keeping a sharp eye out for icebergs," Hammad said.

The sun had set and no moon had come to take its place. I wondered how the men would be able to see anything in the dark, much less icebergs.

By the time Hammad returned me to the suite, the Harpers had roused themselves and were already dressed for dinner. Henry was fastening the clasp at the back of Myra's jeweled necklace.

"Will you be a dear, Hammad, and take charge of Sunny this evening?" Myra asked. "Harry Widener's honoring Captain Smith at dinner tonight, and we daren't miss it."

Hammad and I retired to his room. There, all he seemed able to do was pace.

That's a perfectly charming path you're wearing in this posh carpet, my eyes told him.

The blare of a bugle brought his trail-blazing to a halt. A moment later, there was a knock on the door and the steward delivered Hammad's dinner tray. It smelled delectable. With a flourish, the steward lifted the silver lid from the plate. And there was rich, creamy gravy on the meat!

"Enjoy your meal," said the steward as he bowed his way out the door.

Oh, you can be sure we will, my eyes told him.

Outside in the hallway, it had grown quite noisy. Hammad cracked the door and we both looked out.

The first-class passengers were exiting their suites for the dining saloon. One always knew, from the call of the bugle, when it was mealtime aboard the *Titanic.* Even the richest passengers perked up their ears and slavered, hungry as hounds.

Like Henry and Myra, everyone was dressed to the nines. The men wore tuxedos and black ties. The ladies, their finest gowns. They were draped with fine furs and they dripped with jewels.

Hammad returned to his dinner tray and stared at it bleakly.

I'd be happy to help you clean your plate, I hinted with a faint growl. But, alas, the man pushed the plate away and reached for his coat. Oh joy! Another airing.

Up on the boat deck, Hammad passed the radio room and paused in the doorway. What was our man thinking? Maybe he wished to send a wire to his brother, Said: *Having a wonderful time! Wish you were here!*

The man clicking the key was Mr. Bride, the previously snoring wireman. His pile of messages was as high as ever. He looked up at us briefly, then returned to his work. Hammad heaved a deep sigh and walked on.

We made our way forward toward the bridge. The wind whistled through the rigging. It was biting cold. The air glittered with tiny little bits of ice. Thank goodness we returned to the lower decks before my tongue froze and whiskers grew icicles.

Meanwhile, back on D Deck, the stained glass windows of the dining saloon glowed cheerily. Inside, I thought I could hear the clinking of heavy flatware against china and the tinkling of crystal glasses. I could almost taste the delicious fare: oysters, filet mignon, lamb, roast duckling, squab, and Lily's personal favorite: pâté de foie gras.

We walked on. It was pitch dark now. But that did not stop Hammad from hugging the rails and searching the water for icebergs. By the time we made a second pass of the dining saloon, the room had all but emptied. Waiters and busboys would be clearing away the dessert plates. My nose twitched at the aromas of everything that I might have tasted.

By now, all but a few of the passengers had had the good sense to retire to their rooms. Only three people other than Hammad were game enough to brave the cold night. They sat in deck chairs murmuring to one another, wrapped in blankets.

Hammad climbed to the promenade deck and stood at the port-side rail. The wind had died back and the ocean was as smooth as glass now. I felt a bit drowsy. Far beneath us, the engines rumbled like the belly of a contented beast. The stars were so bright and so close, I found myself reaching out a lazy tongue to lick them.

Just then, a watchman in the crow's nest gave a

quick shout. I sat bolt upright in Hammad's arms.

What's going on? I yipped.

I felt the engines grinding and the ship swinging about.

Hammad ran with me to the starboard rail. He staggered backward as a pale mass passed swiftly by. It was like the white wall of a tunnel and our ship was a railroad train too broad to fit through it. I heard a crunch. Then a rough scraping sound against the side of the vessel. It rattled the glass of all two thousand portholes.

From the bridge, an alarm pierced the air.

Somewhere, I heard boots hit the deck running. Men spoke in voices of shock and disbelief.

The *Titanic* had just hit something. And I knew deep in my doggie heart just what that something was.

A giant iceberg!

SUNDAY, APRIL 14, 11:45 P.M., THE BOAT DECK

The engines stopped abruptly. An eerie silence settled as the ship drifted. Inside the lounge, the men who had been playing cards now looked up. One came out on deck, joining the other passengers who had begun to pop out from below. Some wore their evening clothes. Others had thrown on coats over their pajamas. The question on everyone's lips was, "Why have we stopped?"

The stewards all rushed off to the bridge to find the answer.

One of them said in passing, "I don't suppose it's much. I expect we'll be back underway in an hour or so."

"All the more time to win money at cards," one of the players joked.

John Jacob Astor came up from below. "What seems to be the problem?" he asked.

"It's nothing," said another man. "They say it's probably an iceberg. We've stopped to avoid hitting it."

"Very sensible," said Astor. "Madeleine will be happy to hear it's nothing serious. I must tell her." He disappeared back below.

One of the players said, "Say, I've never seen an iceberg, have you?"

"No—let's go take a look!" said his friend.

In a spirit of adventure, they went off in search of icebergs. "Perhaps I can get a chip off of it for my drink," one said with a laugh.

I felt the engines start up again, so I assumed all was well and we were underway.

A few curious passengers chose to stay up on deck in the warmth of the lounge. But most returned to their rooms. It was late and the night, as I have said, was bitter cold.

"Nothing serious" seemed to be the general thinking. But that was not what Hammad thought, judging from the wild beating of his heart.

"I must warn the Harpers," he said.

On our way to the stairs, we were drawn to a crowd lined up along the rail.

Below us, scattered chunks of ice lay on the third-class well deck. A group of boys were slipping and sliding around. They laughed and shouted, tossed pieces to each other and kicked them.

I spotted Frankie among them. I gave out a shrill yip but he didn't hear me. I willed him to look up so I could tell him, *Trust me, lad—this is no time for ice hockey.*

When Hammad turned away, we saw one of the first-class passengers holding a small piece of ice. "I'm bringing it to New York as a souvenir," he said. "There's plenty of it down there on the deck. Go help yourself."

But we weren't interested in ice. We had to warn the Harpers.

We were just going below, when a deafening roar filled the air as trapped steam escaped from somewhere nearby. I heard people up on deck scream with fear. Hammad hastened his pace.

Down on D Deck, stewards were rushing up and down the long hallway, knocking on doors to reassure passengers that there was no need for alarm.

Hammad knocked on the Harpers' stateroom door.

"What is it now?" Myra asked as she answered. "Oh," she said. "It's you. I thought you were the steward come to tell us once again that there is nothing to worry about."

"Madam," said Hammad. "I believe there is every reason for concern. There is no doubt we have hit an iceberg. I have seen the evidence of it with my own eyes. There are actual chunks of ice on the well deck."

She waved this away. "The *Titanic* could hit a dozen icebergs and still remain afloat."

A moment later, the steward reappeared at the door. "The captain has ordered all ladies on deck. With life belts."

"But this is absurd," Myra protested. "Moments ago, you told me there's nothing to worry about. Now you say I must put on my life belt? What is the meaning of this?"

"Madam, it's just a formality, but it's captain's orders."

Myra went to tell Henry. He came out of his room still in his white shirt and black trousers.

"I'll go up with you, darling," he offered.

"I, too, will go," said Hammad.

We waited in the parlor as the Harpers put on coats and hats and gloves and, as the last layer, their life belts.

Myra looked at herself in the wardrobe mirror and sighed. "I look frightfully dowdy."

Henry said, "No matter, dear. Everyone will be wearing them. It's captain's orders."

"Come to Mummy," Myra said, and held out

her arms for me. After hours of suffering Hammad's nervous grip, her arms were comforting and soft. Unlike Hammad, she was not worried. Not yet, at least.

Out in the hall, we were joined by a river of first-class passengers streaming toward the stairway to the upper decks. They grumbled and complained. Some walked stiffly owing to the many layers of clothing they had put on to keep warm. Others wore their life belts over their bathrobes. Still others had refused to wear their life belts at all. A woman stopped a steward and asked him to run back and fetch her jewelry.

"Don't bother," her husband said. "It'll still be there when we return to our rooms."

"What a load of nonsense," said another man.

The first-class passengers gathered up on the promenade deck. Down on the lower decks, the second- and third-class passengers gathered, too. Everyone waited patiently for news from the captain. Last seen, he was in the company of Thomas Andrews as they ran down to the engine room.

It was so cold on the promenade deck that passengers crowded into the first-class lounge. Avoiding the crush, the Harpers took refuge up on the boat deck in the gymnasium. The Astors were already there, sitting side by side on the electric horses. They looked as if they expected, any second now, to ride off into the frozen night.

"I keep telling Madeleine she has nothing to worry about," said Astor.

Mrs. Astor plucked at his sleeve and sniffed back tears.

"I've been amusing her by showing her what's inside these things."

With his penknife he had made a small cut in a

life belt to show her the cork stuffing inside.

I could not help but wonder, had anyone thought to provide us dogs with life belts? When I thought of my friends over in the kennel, I felt a twinge of guilt. Was anyone looking out for them? Or was the butcher caught up in other matters now? Like strapping on his own life belt?

I gave off a startled little bark as I distinctly felt the ship list to the port side.

"Hush, Sunny. Mummy's got you."

Fat lot of good that will do me on a sinking ship, I growled.

We heard thumping and shouting all around us. The Astors and the Harpers and Hammad and I left the warmth of the gym to investigate.

The area by the lifeboats teemed with seamen, stewards, firemen, and chefs. The men were tearing the canvas off the lifeboats. They were clearing masts and laying in lanterns and tins of biscuits.

"I'll be dashed," said Henry. "It looks like they mean business, no?"

"It's probably just a drill," said Astor. "Besides, anyone can see we are safer here than in that flimsy little boat."

A man began to turn a crank. Pulleys squealed. A boat swung free of the ship and hung out high over the water.

Musical instruments began to tune up in the lounge. The ship's bandmaster and his musicians struck up a ragtime tune. It seemed far too loud and cheerful, considering the occasion. Then again, what was the proper music for boarding lifeboats? A nice brisk march? Handel's *Water Music*? Perhaps a lively chorus of bugles, because these people clearly needed to wake up and pay attention to the seriousness of the situation.

A man wearing a coat with a beaver collar over a heavy woolen suit shouted, "Hear this! Women and children into the boats first!" he said. "Then men . . . but only if there is room."

And dogs? I asked with my eyes. *Say there, good fellow. What about dogs?*

We watched as boat 7 was loaded. What madness was this? Did no one understand the instruction? Men were joining their wives. Mrs. Helen Bishop's husband, Dickinson, climbed in beside her without so much as a howdy-doo. And where was little Frou-Frou? If men were allowed, then surely dogs were, too. I felt a pang of pity for the poor forgotten poodle. Even worse than this, men *without* female companions had begun to board the lifeboats, and none of the officers said one word about it.

"Lower away!" the man in the beaver collar

shouted and the crew obeyed his order.

"Isn't that man helping to load the boats Mr. Ismay?" Henry asked Astor.

"I believe it is. Bruce Ismay, chairman of the White Star Line, himself. Jolly good sport to pitch in and help out like this."

The boat was slowly lowered on ropes down into the sea. It was nearly half-empty, and many in the lifeboat were men. But no one seemed to care!

Mr. Ismay took charge of boat 5 next. Several couples boarded, as well as little Bobo Dodge in the arms of his mother. This boat, too, was only partially filled when Ismay called out, "Anyone else ready to board?"

When no one came forward, he ordered the boat lowered.

Mr. Ismay made a circling motion with his hand. "Lower away! Lower away!" he repeated.

The officer doing the cranking snarled, "If you'll stand clear of the boat, I'll be able to do it! If you want me to lower away that quickly, I'll drown the whole lot of them."

People who witnessed this outburst gasped at the sudden show of bad manners.

Mr. Ismay's face flushed with embarrassment. Without a word he turned to the business of loading the next boat. Henry and Myra—who held me—followed by Hammad, were among the first to step forward when called.

Everyone seemed oddly calm. Ismay said nothing about Henry or Hammad climbing into our boat. Nor did he comment on Mrs. Cardeza's son joining her. Miss Graham from first class had come with her mother and her governess, Miss Shutes. Little Douglas Spedden and both his parents climbed in. But most important of all, Ismay said nothing about me, huddled in Myra's arms.

Had I made the cut? Or perhaps he simply hadn't seen me. After all, I was covered in fur. Myra's coat was made of fur. And she had folded

her gloved hands over my head in an effort, perhaps, to hide me. Then again, it wasn't as if I were some lumbering Great Dane, taking up a seat that a human might have occupied.

Speaking of which, I peered out from between Myra's fingers and caught sight of Darling Boy himself. He was walking the deck at Ann Elizabeth Isham's side. She appeared to be going from boat to boat, begging the officers and mates to allow her to board with her dog. After the last officer had shaken his head, Ann walked proudly away from the boats. Would she remain on the ship with her Great Dane?

It alarmed me when a band of brawny stokers climbed on board our boat. If they were here with us, then who was keeping the ship's furnace fires burning?

And where, blast it all, was Frankie? I knew he

could take care of himself, but I was still worried.

Just as our boat swung over the side, a sudden burst of flame filled the sky. All eyes looked up.

"Distress rockets," said Henry. "They'll alert nearby ships to come to our aid. Not that we need it. We'll probably just bob around a bit and then get back on the *Titanic*."

"I heard someone say we'll need passes to get back on the ship after this is over," said Myra. "I wonder who will be handing them out."

The stokers stared at the Harpers as if they'd gone mad.

"I never thought I'd see the day . . . ," said one of them, his eyes filling with tears.

"Having to dowse all of them furnace fires, only three days out."

"And all them watertight chambers . . . filling up and overflowing."

"I heard Mr. Thomas Andrews himself say it's just a matter of time. The starboard side is full of gashes, and she's taking on tons of water."

"Oh, she's goin' down fast, she is."

As Ismay ordered our boat to be lowered, I imagined the vast engine room flooding with seawater, sloshing about the feet of the remaining greasers and the stokers.

Our boat was halfway down the side of the ship, when Myra sat up tall. "Henry!" she cried out. "You've forgotten your best bowler hat."

But Henry, for whom the stokers' talk had finally sunk in, reached for Myra and drew her close. "Blast the bowler hat, my darling," he whispered. "The *Titanic* is sinking!"

Monday, April 15, 12:50 a.m., the Sinking

The stokers rowed us quickly away from the *Titanic*. Putting their backs into it, they dearly wanted to get our little boat as far away from the sinking ship as possible.

With the *Titanic*'s engines killed, sound carried as clear as a bell over the water. My ears twitched as I heard officers barking orders, people arguing and shouting, and the unmistakable deep rumble of a

Great Dane's bark. It was the dear boy himself.

"Look!" cried out Miss Shutes, the governess, as she pointed.

I nosed away Myra's hands and stood up in her lap to see. A line of third-class passengers on the well deck were crawling up the baggage crane and trying to make their way onto the promenade deck. Yesterday, when Frankie had performed this stunt, it had been a lark. Tonight, it was a desperate effort to scramble up to the lifeboats. From where I sat, it looked as if some of the people at the rails were beating them back while others were trying to help them up.

"They're swatting them like . . . flies!" Miss Graham said as the climbers fell back onto the well deck.

I heard the sharp crack of a pistol. A sudden silence followed. Water sloshed against the walls of our boat. Then the noise aboard the *Titanic* built again as people crowded the boat deck and more lifeboats swung down into the water.

Myra sat, as if frozen with eyes shut, listening. To watch was too much for her.

The other women in our boat were bolder. They passed around a set of glasses. Like ladies at the opera, each took her turn, peering at the goings-on aboard the ship.

Mrs. Cardeza reported: "I see Madeleine Astor boarding a lifeboat now."

"Oh, good," said Myra. "Is John with her?"

"He has just embraced her and backed away from the boat."

"You mean, John's not boarding?" Myra asked in astonishment.

"Of course not, my dear," said Henry wearily. "He's too much of a gentleman, would be my guess. Women and children first—and all that."

"He'll probably get on one of the later boats," Myra said.

"Is it my imagination," said Mrs. Cardeza, "or is the ship riding rather low in the water?"

"There's Mrs. Isidor Straus!" said Miss Graham. "She's helping her maid get on the boat. How very thoughtful of her. Now it looks like she, herself, is backing away from the boat. I believe she's refused to leave without her husband. How is that for true love?"

"Looks like they're enforcing the rules now. Women and children only," said Henry. "No men."

"I'm glad I didn't have to make that choice," Myra said softly, squeezing Henry's hand.

I watched as the loading of lifeboats seemed to speed up.

Smaller boats were dropping into the water

now. Unlike the earlier ones, these were filled to overflowing. The boats, large and small, were rapidly moving away from the *Titanic* in all directions. We watched as one of the collapsibles slipped its lines and slid down the slanting deck into the water, landing upside down. What a waste!

People stood lined up along the rails of the great ship. Among them I thought I saw many third-class passengers. I searched for Frankie. I also saw almost as many first-class passengers: Ben Guggenheim with his manservant, the Strauses, Arthur Ryerson, George Widener and his son, Harry. Meanwhile, the lights of the ship blazed and the band played on. All was calm and normal, except that water was rushing in through the large portholes on C Deck.

As the ship continued to sink, its bow started to dip down into the water and the stern rose up higher into the air.

My ears pricked. I heard dogs barking! Someone must have let them out of the kennel. Then I saw them, running up and down the slanting deck—Kitty and Chow and Dog and Guy and the Carter family dogs. They were all dashing about in search of their human companions.

"Poor things!" Miss Shutes whispered tearfully. "They don't understand what's happening."

"Perhaps they'll be all right on their own," said Mrs. Cardeza. "Dogs are good swimmers, after all."

"I'd be surprised if anyone—man or beast—could survive in this water," said one of the stokers.

People were beginning to leap from the deck of the sinking ship into the sea. The distance to the water was much shorter now. The jumpers landed with a splash, crying out as the cold hit them. Suddenly, the sea was filled with people bobbing about in their life belts. They clung to each other and to

deck chairs and cushions—anything that floated.

"We should row over and lend a hand," Mrs. Cardeza said. "We have room aboard for some of these poor people in the water."

"We can't risk it. They might swamp us," one of the stokers said, "and then we'd all be sunk."

No one said anything. The poop deck—where

once the third-class children had romped and played, where the boys had given us dogs our airing, where Hammad and I stood only hours ago—was almost completely underwater now.

I heard shouts of encouragement as the people on one lifeboat dragged a few of the swimmers out of the water.

On board the ship, the ragtime music stopped. I heard the bandmaster tap his baton. The band struck up a solemn hymn.

As the bow dipped further, a giant wave began to build. It broke over the deck, sending the crowd running up the tilting deck away from the foaming, rushing water. People clung to the rails. Others were swept into the sea. The crow's-nest mast, once the highest point on the ship, had sunk so low that the lookout platform was nearly level with the water.

People could no longer keep their footing on the steeply angled stern deck. They slipped and slid and fell away into the sea. The black ocean teemed with bodies and furniture and machinery. Eerily, the lights in the submerged decks still glowed dully under the water.

As the stern rose ever higher into the air, all

manner of objects rained down upon the ocean: plates and plants and chairs and trunks. The forward funnel toppled and crashed into the sea in a shower of sparks.

The *Titanic* now heaved stern first into the air, black against the starry sky. Its giant rudder and three propellers dripped with water and seaweed. Then, with a deep sigh of defeat, it sank down into the water and disappeared from sight.

In the silence that followed, I heard praying and weeping. I am not ashamed to say that I was among those whimpering. I wept for the loss of my fellow passengers, both human and animal. I also mourned the *Titanic,* the ship whose smug and boastful builders, crew, and passengers all believed it could never possibly sink.

But sink it had.

MONDAY, APRIL 15, 2:15 A.M.,
THE LIFEBOATS

The night fell silent. The only sounds I heard were the slapping of the oars and the sloshing of the water against the sides of the boats. The ocean seemed strangely calm. It was as if, now that it had swallowed the *Titanic* whole, it could settle down for a good night's sleep.

I looked up. I saw small rockets streaking

through the night sky. Then I heard someone whisper, "Shooting stars. Have you ever seen so many?"

On the breast of the vast ocean, our vessels seemed impossibly tiny. The mates strove to keep the boats near one another by lashing some of them together. The oarsmen—and a few oarswomen—all rowed hard toward some bright point on the horizon that might not even have been there.

One lifeboat had flipped over, its passengers clinging desperately to the hull.

In time, the talk among the lifeboat passengers grew livelier.

A woman offered a blanket to comfort a crying baby. A man passed around a flask of spirits. I even heard scattered laughter. I found that my own tail, however faintly, began to wag. Dire as the situation was, you can't keep a good dog down.

I sat tall in Myra's lap and searched every boat with my eyes for some sign of Frankie. Had any of the other dogs survived the sinking?

One of the stokers rowing our boat knocked off to rest. Hammad took over. Now that the worst had happened, Hammad seemed oddly lively and eager to carry his weight.

People shouted from boat to boat. Everyone wondered what had become of Captain Smith.

"He went down with the ship," said one of the mates.

"I spied him swimming away from the wreck," someone else said.

"We saw him plain as day," said another. "He asked if he could come on board, but we had to tell him no. We had no room. He wished us Godspeed and swam off into the night. That was the last I saw of him."

From the direction of the overturned collapsible, to which several men clung, a man said, "Captain Smith and I were among the last to leave."

"Say, were you able to get word out, Mr. Bride?" one of our boat mates asked him.

The wireman explained that he was on the radio up until the very last minute, when the captain ordered him to abandon ship. He was able to get a distress call out to every ship in the area. "The *Olympic*, the *Baltic*, and the *Carpathia* are the closest to us," he said. Before he signed off, he gave them our position and they gave him theirs. "The *Carpathia*'s man told me they were already on their way, full speed ahead. Their captain said it would be four hours. I told him, 'Come as quickly as possible, old man; the engine room is filling up to the boilers.' That was the last message I got out."

As the sky began to lighten toward morning,

the sea grew angry and choppy. I was terrified to see that we were surrounded by floating ice. Many pieces were no bigger than my head, but a few towered over the lifeboats. The rowers had to struggle not to collide with them.

Little Douglas Spedden said, "Oh, look at the beautiful North Pole . . . with no Santa Claus!"

The freezing waves broke over the sides of our boat. A splash of icy sea spray hit me in the face. I shivered and sneezed. Myra, in spite of her fur coat, shook as if with a fever. People had fallen silent again. They were too cold and tired to speak. Some people moaned as they cradled broken limbs or cracked heads. Some lay still.

I worried that the Atlantic Ocean seemed vast and never-ending. Would anyone ever be able to find us out here?

Sometime before dawn, we saw fiery trails

streaking the distant sky. Still more shooting stars?

"They're rockets!" one of the stokers shouted joyfully. "The rescue ship has set off rockets . . . to let us know they're on the way."

It wasn't long before we saw a single smoke-stack on the horizon, steaming its way toward us. Even from a distance, I could see it was making rapid headway. Down in the engine room, its stokers must have been pouring on the coal.

People in the lifeboats gave out a cheer.

"It's the *Carpathia,* all right," one of the officers said. "I'd know that rusty old tub anywhere."

Myra looked up wearily. "It's got only one smokestack. The *Titanic* had four."

"And where are those smokestacks now, Myra?" Henry said sadly. "On the bottom of the North Atlantic, that's where."

The oarsmen in every boat began to row with

renewed vigor. Our little fleet moved steadily forward to meet the *Carpathia.* As we got closer, a few passengers stood up and waved their arms or hats. Mates or officers shouted at them to sit down or risk overturning the boats.

One old man set a newspaper on fire and held it high, trailing sparks.

"We're here! We're here!" he shouted in a hoarse voice.

Even I, who had until now gone out of my way not to attract attention, stood up in Myra's lap and started barking my fool head off.

Huzzah! We were saved!

MONDAY, APRIL 15, THE *CARPATHIA*

Our rescue ship floated upon an ocean of shattered ice, for as far as the eye could see. In the early hours of that fateful morning, the crew of the *Carpathia* were as gallant as they were efficient. One after another, they made fast the lifeboats to its side. Then they assisted the passengers in climbing up rope ladders or shimmying up lines to board. Ladies and the wounded were hoisted up on swings. Children were hauled up, special delivery, in canvas sacks.

The first thing I noticed was that this vessel was ever so much smaller and drabber than the sunken one. Only days ago, as I boarded that ill-fated ship, I noticed that even its hull seemed to gleam, so new and beautiful was it.

The *Carpathia*'s hull, on the other paw, was scarred and dented. But at that moment, it was the most gorgeous thing I had ever laid eyes on. This old ship had seen many a voyage over the years. No doubt, this one would be its most memorable. Mine, too, I don't mind saying.

As one lifeboat was made fast to the *Carpathia*'s hull, a lady screamed out, "The boat has gone down with everyone on board!"

The mate on her lifeboat cut her off. "Shut up!" And shut up she did, just as quickly as if someone had stuck a cork in her mouth.

And then there was the woman on our own

boat when it came time for us to board. None of us had paid her very much mind. All the while we had been floating, she had lain motionless in the bottom of the boat in her nightgown and robe. When someone scrambled over her body to get to the ladder, this creature rose up like a wraith and pointed a finger.

"That woman just stepped on my stomach!" she screeched.

Her mouth, too, was quickly corked.

It was as if the slightest outburst might set us all to raving. I came up quite peacefully in a swing on Myra's lap, Myra holding me in a hammerlock. But I didn't care, so grateful was I to be off that flimsy little craft.

Henry followed Myra, shimmying up a line and stepping on deck as cool as you please. He recognized a friend among the *Carpathia*'s passengers.

"Louis, old man," he said, strolling over to the chap as if they were meeting up at the club, "how do you keep yourself so young?"

Awaiting us on deck were stacks of blankets, pots of soup and coffee, and crates of clothes donated by the *Carpathia's* passengers, both first class and steerage. A steward was there to greet each and every survivor with a blanket, a set of dry clothing, and a cup of something hot to drink. Another steward marked down on a clipboard the name and the traveling class of each new arrival.

The next boat delivered the chairman of the White Star Line, Mr. Ismay himself. All hands rushed to give him the royal treatment. They offered him clothing, food, medicines. But he would have none of it.

"Just show me to a room and leave me in peace," said the man.

He looked like a man who had lost everything. And perhaps he had.

Myra thrust me at Hammad as she and Henry went off to a stateroom donated by one of the first-class passengers.

The *Carpathia*'s lounge was crowded with survivors. Hammad took a blanket and rubbed my frozen fur dry. A little brushing and I'd be ready for the dog show that was to have taken place this morning.

Staff were handing out cups of hot soup. Hammad set down a bowl for me and I lapped at it with surprising gusto. At least I still had my appetite. My chilled insides began to warm. Nearby, one of the galley workers whispered to a stoker, "Where's the rest? We expected so many more of you."

"They all went down with the ship," said the stoker with a shake of his head.

People huddled in groups, not for conversation so much as for comfort and warmth. Sad souls wandered, searching for wives, husbands, children, friends—whoever they may have been, lost in the confusion. There were a few joyful reunions. But far more often, when the search proved fruitless, the tears flowed.

One woman looked at me and burst into tears. "They could save a dog, but not my husband?"

Take it easy, lady, I growled. *Is it my fault I'm lap-size?*

A kind man agreed with me. "There, there," he said as he led the lady off. "It's not the poor doggie's fault."

I saw that the Carter family had reunited. The boy, Billy, had been forced to wear a woman's flowery hat so he could sneak a seat on an all-women boat. It looked rather becoming on him, I must say. But he flung down the hat and stomped on it when his father told him that he had failed to save the family dogs.

"You lied. You said you'd bring them in a later boat!" Billy shouted.

"It just wasn't possible, son. There wasn't room for all the people, much less the dogs."

As if on cue, all eyes went to me. I stopped lapping my soup.

Don't look at me. I didn't ask to be saved, I tried to tell them with my eyes. *Not that I'm complaining, mind you. I love life as much as the next dog.*

And that's when I realized, I *did* love life. I was *glad* to be alive. As if it had a mind of its own, my tail began to wag as I caught sight of Mrs. Rothschild with her Pomeranian nestled in her lap. So I wasn't the only canine survivor! Then I saw Mrs. Bishop sitting hunched on a bench, her lap empty where Frou-Frou ought to have been. My tail drooped.

The woman sitting next to her had the same thought. "Frou-Frou didn't make it?"

Mrs. Bishop wept. "She's gone. I left her in the cabin. As I was leaving, she latched on to me with her little teeth. She begged to come with me. I told her she must stay. I was so sure I'd be back, you see. It would have been so easy for me to carry

125

her in my arms. But by the time I realized the ship was doomed, they wouldn't let me go back to the room. They said it was too dangerous. Myra Harper thought to bring her Peke with her. And Mrs. Rothschild wrapped her little Pom in a blanket and convinced everyone it was a human baby."

My soup bowl now empty, I crawled back into Hammad's lap, craving human warmth.

"I see Sunny's still with us," Miss Hays said, sitting down next to Hammad. Lily lay shivering in her arms. Once again, my heart did a little jig. That made three of us dogs who had escaped.

Miss Hays leaned in to my Egyptian friend. "Tell me, Mr. Hassat. Have Myra and Henry . . . ?"

Hammad nodded. "They are safe. We were able to board the third lifeboat."

As she expressed her relief, I said to the still-jittery Mamzelle Lily, *Hail, fellow survivor.*

What an absolument beastly voyage. I knew it was a terrible mistake to ever leave Paris. Dommage!

At least you're alive, I told her, *which is more than I can say for the others.*

Her eyes widened. *Really? You mean Darling Boy and Dog and Guy and . . . ?*

Kitty and Frou-Frou and Chow and both the Carter dogs. . . . I nodded sadly. *Down with the ship, as the saying goes.*

Dommage, she said. *It is too, too sad.*

I imagine they're crossing that golden bridge to the great doggie beyond right about now, I said.

Just then, I heard a familiar voice: "Little lion dog! So ye made it after all!"

I would have known that voice anywhere. I leapt to my feet and I looked around. At first glance, I didn't recognize my friend. Gone were the short pants, the shabby jacket, and the rakish cap. He was dressed almost clownishly, in a grown man's waistcoat and starched white shirt. The too-long trousers puddled about his feet. He looked like a funny little old man. And yet he was a sight to make my heart take wing.

Frankie! I danced with happiness and barked with joy. *Frankie, me boy!*

Frankie knelt and put his face close to mine. He had a mean-looking bruise on his forehead. I licked it gently. *You're hurt.*

"Don't worry about me, little lion dog. I made out fine . . . compared to some."

Hammad looked upon our little reunion in puzzlement. "Young man, it seems that you and Sunny are old friends."

Frankie grinned. "So *that's* his name. It fits him, what with them big eyes and that smiley mouth and all. I call him me little lion dog. Him and me got acquainted back there . . . on board the ship."

"I am glad you are alive and well, young man," Hammad said, "and it appears Sunny is, too."

"I thought I was a goner. Found meself paddling around in the briny. I once fell into the river Farset and nearly froze me fingers off, but this water was a proper ice bath, it was, colder than a polar bear's nose. Lucky for me, me uncles and me dad came and dragged me and my sister onto a raft they'd lashed together from deck chairs. It was third class all the way."

"It is a miracle we are here," Hammad said solemnly. "You will excuse us now, please, Miss Hays, young man. I must take Sunny to see his mistress. She will be wanting to keep her little fellow close."

"Can't say as I blame her. He's a great little doggie. See you around, Sunny," Frankie said. He reached out a finger and touched my nose.

I licked his finger. It tasted of the ocean.

See you around, Frankie. Good luck to you.

"Who knows?" Frankie said, backing away. "Maybe we'll meet up again someday . . . on American soil."

Three days later, I was standing at the rail with Hammad as we approached New York City, our port of entry. In the flurry of activity that surrounded us, Hammad stood quite still. His dark eyes were fixed on the big statue in the harbor of a lady holding up a torch.

I began to hear a honking sound, like the biggest flock of geese ever. A small fleet of boats had come to greet us and escort us to the dock. They surrounded us, each one tooting its horn for all it was worth. On their decks, crew and passengers cheered and waved at us. I always say, there's

nothing like a warm welcome to set a dog's tail
to wagging.

The honking was soon followed by roaring.
At first, I thought a storm might have blown up.

And then I saw that the *Carpathia* was nearing a massive crowd of humans, standing on the dock. The welcome we were receiving was downright thunderous.

Hammad fell in behind the Harpers as they joined the stream of passengers going down the gangplank and into the crowd. Among them, reporters shouted questions through megaphones. Most were, frankly, rather silly:

"How does it feel to be alive?"

And "Will you ever set foot on a White Star Line ship again?"

Or, most insulting of all, "I see they managed to save a little dog. But not over one thousand human beings. How do you feel about that?"

The Harpers found themselves at the center of attention. Friends and reporters flocked around the couple, eagerly wanting to hear their story.

Much to my relief, for my head was beginning to spin, Hammad, with me in his arms, managed to slip away.

After making several inquiries, he found the marconiman's office on the dock. The wireman, just like Mr. Bride, had a fat stack of messages. They were messages from the survivors to their loved ones.

The man looked up from his work. "What can I do for you, young man?"

"I would like to send a wire to my brother," Hammad said. He held out a slip of paper.

The man took it and read out loud:

> To Said Hassat
>
> Mena House
>
> Cairo, Egypt
>
> All safe
>
> Hammad

Safe. Yes, that about summed it up. We were among the fortunate few. Said's prediction had come all too true.

"You're one of the lucky ones," the wireman told my serious friend. "And may all the others—passengers and crew—rest in peace."

And dogs, too, my friend, I said with my eyes. *Dogs, too.*

As we walked away from the wire office, I thought that the one big lesson I had learned from this voyage was to savor each precious day as if it were my last. I wouldn't be surprised if it was a lesson that Hammad, and all the other survivors, had carried away with them from that fateful night.

And savor it I would, indeed—every single bite of it. With or without gravy.

APPENDIX

The Unsinkable Ship

The sinking of the RMS *Titanic* is the stuff of legend. Disasters at sea have always captured the public imagination. But what makes the *Titanic*'s fate even more fascinating—and horrific—was that the vessel was designed, built, and advertised to be unsinkable. Not only did it sink, but it did so barely six days into its maiden voyage—with some of the world's wealthiest and most prominent citizens on board.

At its helm was Captain Edward John Smith, a highly regarded commanding officer of the White Star Line fleet. The man was experienced and confident—perhaps too much so. Before the maiden voyage of another White Star Line ship, he had said, "I cannot imagine any condition which could cause a ship to founder. I cannot conceive of any vital disaster happening to this vessel. Modern shipbuilding has gone beyond that."

Another man had the same belief. He was the managing director of the White Star Line, J. Bruce Ismay. In 1907, Ismay commissioned the Belfast firm of Harland & Wolff to build the *Titanic,* along with two sister ships. At 882 feet in length and ten decks high, it was, at the time, the largest human-made moving object on earth. The anchor alone was so big and heavy that it took twenty horses to carry it.

At least three thousand men worked six days a week for nearly two years to construct the hull. It was a triple-screw vessel, with three powerful propellers turned by two different kinds of engines, all of which were driven by the steam created by 159 furnaces. The ship had a double bottom and sixteen watertight compartments designed to guarantee flotation.

After the ship's body was built, a team of three thousand master carpenters, electricians, painters, and designers took over. The decor and furnishings were inspired by some of the world's most luxurious hotels. The Grand Staircase—oak paneled and decorated with paintings and gilded cherubs—extended down six of the ship's ten decks. It was intended for the use of first-class passengers only. There was a second, less elegant staircase (the one used by Frankie and Sunny), but that, too, was restricted. The rule in those days, on land as on the sea, was that the classes did not mingle.

On the boat deck, which was uppermost, were fourteen wooden lifeboats, two emergency cutters, and four collapsible boats, with room for 1,178 people. While this was insufficient to carry the *Titanic*'s more than twenty-two hundred passengers, it did exceed the number of lifeboats required by law at the time.

Before the disaster, the *Titanic* received about six iceberg warnings from other ships. The *Titanic*'s radio operators, or marconimen, were so busy sending out greetings from *Titanic* passengers, however, that not all of these warnings reached the captain or his men on the bridge, who were piloting the vessel.

The iceberg that sank the ship was spotted three days into the voyage, about 11:40 on the evening of April 14, 1912, by lookout Frederick Fleet. It was seventy-five feet tall and had calved, or broken off, from a glacier in Greenland. First Officer William Murdoch, having seen the iceberg, ordered the ship to turn, but it was too late. Only seconds later, the collision occurred. Some people say that had the ship not started to turn but instead hit the iceberg straight on, it might have survived. But who can really say for certain?

When extensive damage was reported to the captain, who was not on the bridge when it occurred, he directed the crew to summon passengers to assemble, with life belts, and to prepare the lifeboats. Then he went below with the ship's designer, Thomas Andrews, to inspect the damage firsthand. The ocean was pouring in through several gashes in the starboard, or right-hand side of the ship when facing forward. Within minutes, the *Titanic* had taken on over a million gallons. The watertight compartments were rapidly filling up. The compartments had been designed with no seal at the top. Once filled, they overflowed into the next one. Smith went above and gave the order to load the lifeboats. "Women and children first," he instructed.

Despite the captain's order, quite a few men boarded the lifeboats. And many of the lifeboats were only half filled to capacity before launching. No one knows why the crew of the *Titanic* did such a poor job following orders. Did they panic? Was it because the captain had canceled the lifeboat drill that very morning? Were people refusing to board, believing that the *Titanic* would never sink? Many third-class passengers didn't speak English and failed to understand the gravity of the situation until it was too late.

The fact remains that of the 2,229 passengers on board, the total number of survivors was 713— although we will never know for sure.

At 2:20 on the morning of April 15, less than

three hours after the collision, the *Titanic* sank from sight. Regarding the *Titanic*'s final moments, eyewitness testimonies differ. Some survivors claim they saw it crack in two before sinking. Others said it broke into four pieces, while still others saw it sink intact. The night was pitch black, and the ship was surrounded by lifeboats filled with people who viewed the event from different angles. We will never know for sure.

Great disasters tend to give rise to great reform, and the *Titanic* sinking was no different. The Radio Act of 1912—enacted within four months after the sinking—stated, among other things, that radio communication on passenger ships had to be open twenty-four hours a day and that there had to be an extra line available to receive distress calls. The Convention for the Safety of Life at Sea, an international agreement signed in 1914, mandated that passenger ships have enough lifeboats to accommodate *all* passengers on board. Lifeboat drills were required, as were regular inspections of lifeboats.

After any disaster, people look to place blame. Some felt it was the captain's fault for speeding through an area known for icebergs. Others felt it was the radiomen's fault for being too busy sending and receiving wires for the passengers to pass along iceberg warnings. Or that it was the designer's fault for not putting caps on the watertight compartments. Whoever or whatever was to blame, the one thing we can say for certain is that hubris was involved.

What is hubris? *Hubris* is a Greek word that means "having too much pride and defying the gods." In Greek tragedy, those guilty of hubris were punished by the gods. It was pure hubris that caused the builders and operators of the *Titanic* to believe that the ship could never, under any circumstances, sink. And yet their unsinkable ship sank.

For more information on *Titanic* facts, history, and people, you can go to these sites:

- titanichistoricalsociety.org
- encyclopedia-titanica.org

Dogs at Sea

Contrary to Sunny's opinion, the *Titanic*'s dog kennel was probably, like every other detail of the ship, nearly perfect. After all, the dogs for whom it was intended belonged to wealthy first-class passengers. Nothing was too good for them, or for their dogs. Apart from walks on the poop deck with the ship's lowliest crew members (probably the boys who cleaned the staterooms), and visits with their human companions on the promenade deck, the dogs spent most of the short voyage in the kennel. The exception to this was Helen Bishop's Frou-Frou, deemed "too dainty" to stay with the larger dogs in the kennel. She was allowed to stay in the Bishops' stateroom, although, ironically, she failed to survive the sinking. Some witnesses claim that the crew really did plan to have a dog show on board. As fate would have it, the *Titanic* sank on the day it was scheduled to take place.

One reporter, probably trying to stir up a fuss, asked Henry Harper about his having saved his dog when so many humans had perished. Harper replied, "There seemed to be lots of room and nobody made any objection." It is probably no coincidence that the three surviving dogs—

a Pekingese and two Pomeranians—were all lap-dogs. Either no one noticed them on the lifeboats because they were so small, or no one objected to their presence because they did not take up a place that might have gone to a human.

Some survivors' accounts indicate that Ann Elizabeth Isham was seen trying to bring her Great Dane onto a lifeboat but that she was repeatedly turned away. She refused to board without him. In the days following the sinking, as legend has it, rescue boats found a woman believed to be her, still clutching the body of her beloved Great Dane.

At some point during the sinking, survivors testified to seeing the kennel dogs running loose on the boat deck. Other witnesses said that someone tied the dogs to a rail. In any case, the unfortunate animals went down with the ship, along with over fifteen hundred people—in one of the greatest peacetime maritime disasters in history.

Did Sunny really have adventures with Frankie? Well, there *was* a nine-year-old Frankie Goldsmith on the third-class passenger list. He was seen monkeying around on a baggage crane and lurking in places he had no business being. He survived to tell a tale that did not include an encounter with a Pekingese, however. Who knows? Maybe he wanted to keep it a secret? (And maybe dogs really do keep diaries!) There was a ship's cat called Jenny. One mate claimed that Jenny was seen to be abandoning the ship in Southampton, with her kittens in her mouth. He claimed this was proof that the cat sensed the coming disaster. Others maintain that Jenny remained on board and that the mate's account was just a superstitious tale.

The History of the Pekingese

When the passenger in the third-class lounge of the *Titanic* said that Sunny was "an aristocrat," he wasn't far off. About two thousand years ago in China, during the Tang dynasty, "lion dogs" were a breed owned only by members of the Chinese imperial family. Royals tucked these dogs up the wide sleeves of their silk coats, hence their other name, sleeve dogs. In fact, sleeve dogs were themselves treated like royalty. Subjects had to bow down to them. And the penalty for removing one from the palace was death.

The dogs were originally bred by Tibetan monks during the time that Buddhism was first coming to China, having spread there in the second century via Indian missionaries. The lion was an important symbol to Buddhists. There being no lions in China, the monks set out to create a miniature lion by breeding the smallest, hairiest dogs they could find to create the lion dog.

The lion dog did not appear in the West until around 1860. During the Second Opium War, when British troops sacked the Chinese palace, they came away with five royal dogs. John Hart Dunne, then a captain of the British Army, gave the smallest one as a gift to Queen Victoria, who named it Looty.

The British upper class took to the little dogs with their flat faces and saucer eyes. Everyone who was anyone wanted one for a lapdog. In 2017, Pekingese ranked eighty-eight on the American Kennel Club list of most popular dogs.

For more information on the history of the

Pekingese, check out this site:

- thepekingeseclubofamerica.net/breed-history.html

Owning a Pekingese

Pekes are noble and intelligent and, like Sunny, just a tad full of themselves. Some people say that this particular breed might not be the best choice for a first dog. They require patient training, proper socialization, and lots of love. They are especially good for apartment dwellers because they don't need a yard or much exercise. They do, however, require daily brushing and grooming. Their long hair tends to mat, tangle, and shed year-round, so owners need to be prepared for lots of dog hair on furniture and clothing. They are also sometimes difficult to housebreak. Lastly, as with any highly bred dog, it is important to obtain one from a responsible breeder.

You can find more information on the breed, as well as links to rescue groups, here:

- akc.org/dog-breeds/pekingese
- pekingesecharitablefoundation.com

Pekingese dog (Can you resist that face?)